Victor Osborne

One Dark Night

Illustrated by Andy Ellis

Victor Osborne

One Dark Night

Illustrated by Andy Ellis

Hippo Books
Scholastic Children's Books
London

For Rupert and Giles, who would ride dragons every night
Victor Osborne

For Dad and Mum
Andy Ellis

Scholastic Children's Books,
Scholastic Publications Ltd,
7-9 Pratt Street, London NW1 0AE, UK

Scholastic Inc.,
730 Broadway, New York, NY 10003, USA

Scholastic Canada Ltd,
123 Newkirk Road, Richmond Hill,
Ontario, Canada L4C 3G5

Ashton Scholastic Pty Ltd,
P O Box 579, Gosford, New South Wales,
Australia

Ashton Scholastic Ltd,
Private Bag 1, Penrose, Auckland,
New Zealand

First published by Scholastic Publications Ltd, 1991
This edition published, 1992

Text copyright © Victor Osborne, 1991
Illustrations copyright © Andy Ellis, 1991

ISBN 0 590 55075 6

Made and printed in Belgium

10 9 8 7 6 5 4 3 2 1

Once upon a stormy night Ben couldn't get to sleep for the growling of a tiger in the garden and the whoosh, whoosh, whooshing of a dragon on the roof.

"Mummy, Mummy, help," he called from under the bedclothes. "There's a tiger outside. And a dragon, too."

Now, if there was anything Ben was afraid of, it was tigers because of their big sharp teeth, and if there was anything else he was afraid of, it was dragons because of their burning breath.

"I'm frightened," he whispered to Floss, the rag patch dog who slept on the bed beside him, and to his other friends, Mew the cat, Earoff the bear, the ladybird called Spots, and Batty who bobbed up and down with outstretched wings on elastic string.

Ben's mummy looked out.

"It's only the wind," she said, kissing him.
"Go to sleep, it's all right."

There was a tremendous crash from the pear tree in
the garden, then a funny sound like a kettle going off
the boil: *Whee-ee-e.*

Ben had to look. He jumped out of bed and ran across the floor to the window and pulled back the curtains.

There in the pear tree, caught in its branches, was — a witch on a motorbike. The motorbike gave a last *whee-ze* as its wheels stopped turning.

An extra strong gust of wind shook the tree, and the motorbike and the witch fell to the ground. Her crash helmet came off revealing spiky blue hair, glowing eyes and a face like a crab's claw about to snap shut.

"Crikey Mikey!" gasped Ben, jumping back as the gust blew the window open with a bang.

The witch picked herself up muttering crossly. She tried to start the bike. *Putter, putter, wheee*, it went in a tired way.

She hitched up her purple dress and kicked the motorbike in a fury, chipping paint off the sign on the fuel tank. The sign had read: 'Spelly Nelly. Wicked Witch. Maker of Horrible Spells.' It now looked like 'Smelly Nelly. Maker of Horrible *Smells.*'!

The dragon on the roof flew past the window and down to the witch to offer its help.

Now Ben thought he knew all about dragons but nobody had ever told him about the ones with two heads. There it sat, a beautiful shiny green and like a normal dragon in every way except that it had two long necks, side by side, with a head on each one.

The witch wasn't surprised. "Oh, thank you kind dragon," she said. "I'm on my way to cast a spell and I'm very late."

"We hope it's a good spell," said the first dragon head.

"We couldn't help you cast a bad spell," said the second head.

"It's the nicest possible spell, my dears," said Spelly Nelly covering up the sign on the motor bike, and she smiled a horrible crabby smile which showed her pointed teeth.

She asked the dragon to whoosh fire, and as it
opened its mouths, she pulled a magic net out of her
sleeve and caught the whooshes just as they popped out.
In a flash she shoved them up the twin exhaust pipes
of the motorbike. Then she jumped on, and with
two bursts of fire and smoke, the motorbike shot into
the air.

"Give me my whooshes back, you wicked witch,"
croaked the dragon in a whisper.

"Heh, heh, heh," cackled the witch. "I fooled you, I'm going to make a really nasty spell to turn all the sweets and chocolates in all the shops in all the world into wriggly worms and creepy slugs."

"Now, to make my nasty spell I need," and Spelly Nelly began to recite:
"Hair of dog and claw of cat,
Stir in too a wing of bat,
Spotty bug, a great bear's hug;

Take them from their bedroom snug.
Before I bake, stir and shake
Then mix 'em with a garden rake!
I wonder where I can find all those things. Hmmm.
But first I need a tiger's growl to make this bike work properly."

Spelly Nelly swooped down on the tiger who was sitting at the end of the garden and opening its mouth to pop in a strawberry. It growled when it saw her, and quick as a flash Spelly Nelly threw her magic net and caught the growl which she stuffed into the engine.

Now the motorbike went *whoosh, whoosh, grow-row-row.*

"We've got to stop the witch before she makes up that terrible spell," said Ben to his friends who had crowded round him by the open window, "or we'll all be in trouble. Come on."

The dragon, who was called Ping Pong, was trying to whoosh, first with one mouth, then the other, and squeezing big fat tears out of his four eyes when nothing happened.

"Cheer up," said Ben, "we'll get the whooshes back for you, but we must catch the witch and stop that spell."

"Climb on my back," said Ping, and Pong said: "Show me which way she went." Ben held on tightly with an arm round each neck, and Floss and Mew and Earoff and Spots and Batty held on tightly behind him as Ping Pong flew up over the pear tree.

It was tremendously exciting. "Woweee," yelled Ben.
"Woof, miaow, rowr, eek, squeak," cried the others.
   Below them they saw the tiger trying to growl, but
making no sound at all, so they shouted: "Follow us to
catch the witch."

"There she is," shouted Ben. And there she was.
Spelly Nelly had stopped by a garden shed to pick up
the rake she needed to mix her spell.

"Quickly," said Ben to Ping Pong, "Take us down
and we'll capture her."

The dragon dived. Ben closed his eyes as they crashed
through the branches of a plum tree onto the
motorbike, smashing it to pieces.

The whooshes burst out of the exhaust pipes, and as
quick as a flash Ping Pong snap-snapped them up.

"That's much better," he snorted loudly, shooting out
two scorching flames.

The tiger jumped over the wall with snarling teeth just in time to catch his growl as the engine fell to bits. The fuel tank flew through the air and hit Spelly Nelly in the tummy like a football.

"Ooof," she screeched, sitting down with a bump beside the smashed motorbike. "I can't fly on that anymore. I'll have to stay here."

"Oh, no you won't," said Ben, "and you can't use my
friends to make your horrible spell, can she?"

"No, she can't," shouted everyone, closing around
the witch in an angry circle. Spelly Nelly screwed up her
frightful face and hissed at them like a snake.
"Hissssss."

Ping Pong went *whoosh, whoosh* and scorched the
soles of the witch's boots. "All right, I won't," she cried,
"but please don't frizzle me to a cinder."

Ben picked up the broken twigs from the plum tree and tied them on to the rake with his dressing-gown cord.

"There, it's as good as a broomstick. Make a spell so you can fly on that."

And that's what Spelly Nelly did, and Ping Pong flew after her, giving a little *whoosh, whoosh* from time to time to make sure she flew far away and never came back.

The tiger took Ben and his friends home on his back, jumping up with them through the open bedroom window.

When they had said goodbye to the tiger and Ben had closed the window and got into bed, he settled his friends around him and asked:

"Are we afraid of
the great uproar
from the dragon and tiger
which rattles the door
as they sing their song
of the witch we saw?
Well, are we afraid?

No! Not any more!

And Ben smiled happily and went to sleep.